One Little Teddy Bear

First published by HarperCollins 1991
First published in Picture Lions 1992

Picture Lions is an imprint of the Children's Division,
part of HarperCollins Publishers Limited,
77-85 Fulham Palace Road, Hammersmith,
London W6 8JB

Printed and bound in Singapore

One Little Teddy Bear

Mark Burgess

PictureLions

An Imprint of HarperCollins*Publishers*

One little teddy bear
Looking for his shoe;
Look inside the wardrobe,
Now there are . . .

Two little teddy bears
Underneath a tree;
Look up in the branches,
Now there are . . .

Three little teddy bears
Dancing on the floor;
Look behind the curtain,
Now there are . . .

Four little teddy bears
Going for a drive;
Open up the sunroof,
Now there are . . .

Five little teddy bears
Doing magic tricks;
Look inside the magic box,
Now there are . . .

Six little teddy bears
Looking up to heaven;
Lift the red umbrella,
Now there are . . .

Seven little teddy bears
Trying hard to skate;
Look behind the holly bush,
Now there are . . .

Eight little teddy bears
Sitting down to dine;
Lift up the tablecloth,
Now there are . . .

Nine little teddy bears
Nearly home again;
Look inside the front door,
Now there are . . .